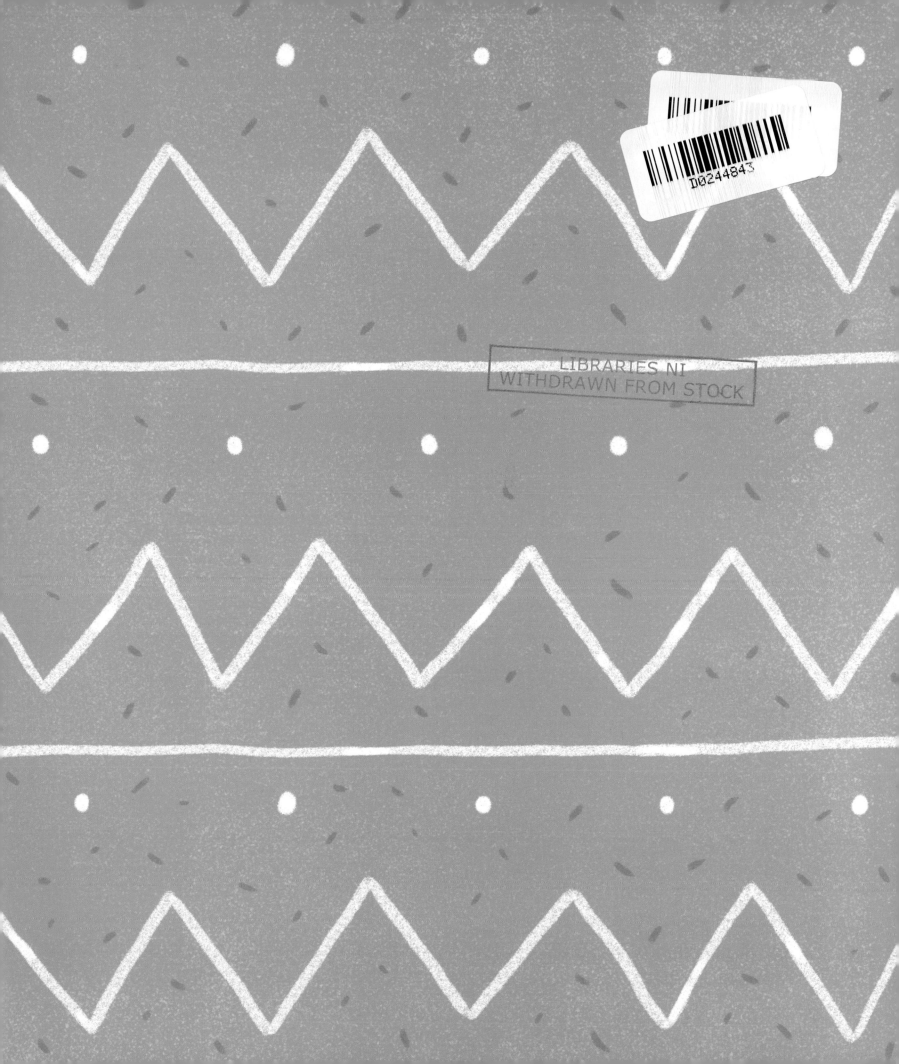

For Mark, thanks for your
belief and support ~ T C

For Laura and my family, thanks for
all the support! Love you, guys ~ T N

LITTLE TIGER PRESS LTD,
an imprint of the Little Tiger Group
1 Coda Studios,
189 Munster Road,
London SW6 6AW
www.littletiger.co.uk

First published in Great Britain 2018
This edition published 2019

Printed in China • LTP/1400/2636/0619

10 9 8 7 6 5 4 3 2 1

The Christmas EXTRAVAGANZA Hotel

TRACEY CORDEROY

TONY NEAL

LITTLE TIGER

LONDON

Far from the busy bustle of town,
Bear was ready for a nice, simple Christmas.
His cosy fire popped and danced,
and his candle cast a golden glow.
But as he opened his favourite book,
he heard a loud

Toot! Toot!

Bear looked up.
"Whoever could that be?"

"Hello!" said a cheery little frog. "I've arrived for my Christmas **EXTRAVAGANZA!** Show me the lights! The tree! The flying reindeer! Let's get Christmas started!"

Frog waved a brochure under Bear's nose.

"The Christmas Extravaganza Hotel?" read Bear.
"I think you've got the wrong place."

"No! No!" Frog tapped the map.
"It's right here, see?"

Bear looked closer. "Oh! Your map's
upside-down. **That** hotel is on
the other side of the world."

"But . . . it CAN'T be!"
wailed Frog. "I had it all
planned – I've even knitted a
hat, look! Now I'll never get
to my hotel in time for
Christmas!"

Bear thought very hard.
"You could always stay with . . .
umm . . . me?" he said kindly.
"I'm going to have a
wonderful Christmas!"

"You ARE?"
Frog brushed his tears away.
"Hurrah!"

He hopped on in, drank a HUGE mug of cocoa,
then dozed off by Bear's cosy fire.
     As Frog slept, Bear flicked through the brochure . . .
"A singing tree?" he gasped. "A supersonic
sleigh ride? Frog won't find that here!"

SUPERSONIC!!
SLEIGH RIDE

SUPER
SONIC!!

But then he looked at the small snoring
bundle, dreaming of a magical Christmas.
"Poor little fellow," whispered Bear.
"Let's see what we can do!"

"Bear! Bear!" called Frog early the next morning.
"Can we please start our Christmas
EXTRAVAGANZA?"
"Of course," yawned Bear.
So Frog checked the brochure . . . "Ooo, so do you have
an all-you-can-eat North Pole breakfast bar?"
"Not exactly," replied Bear. "But we could make iced pastries?"
"Really?? With Christmas sprinkles?
Show me! Show me!!"
Frog cried.

Bear handed him an apron and they started to bake.

And although it wasn't exactly like the brochure, Frog rather liked it!

With breakfast ticked off, Frog looked around.
  "Bear, where is your Christmas tree?" he asked. "My brochure has a BIG one – that sings!"
  Smiling, Bear led Frog outside . . .

"Will this one do?" he asked.
Frog looked up . . . .
and up . . . and UP! "WOW!"

Bear's beautiful tree twinkled with frost.
"And look!" cried Frog as two little robins
hopped about, chirping brightly. "It's even
got interactive singing decorations!
And . . . . SNOW! Do you have a
snow-machine?"
"No! No!" chuckled Bear.
"That's real snow!"

Frog soon found he adored
real snow. And long walks
through the woods.

And picnic lunches!

In the snow Frog
found footprints.
"Let's follow them . . ."
smiled Bear.

And there in the clearing were three **real** reindeer!
"Now we can have a **sleigh ride!!**" whooped Frog.
But Bear shook his head.
"Sorry, these aren't Santa's reindeer," he said.
"And sadly I don't have a sleigh."

But Bear knew **exactly** what Frog would like instead . . .

"Snowball fight! Hurrah!!"
cheered Frog. "And that's
not even in the brochure!"

They played until the sky
turned inky blue.
"And now for the BEST bit!"
Frog exclaimed. "Time to turn on
the Christmas lights!"

He whisked out his brochure
and showed Bear a photo
with string upon string of
lights, flashing away.

Christmas
EXTRAVAGANZA
HOTEL

"Oh," Bear sighed.
His Christmas lights
weren't like those.

Bear hurried home and lit all of his candles.
"W-will these lights do?" he asked.
Frog blinked. They weren't quite the
EXTRAVAGANZA
he'd expected. But Bear had been so kind . . .

"Why . . . y-yes!" spluttered Frog, putting on a big smile.
"So . . . ummmm . . . Christmassy!"

They watched the golden flames in silence.
Then suddenly Bear's eyes lit up.
"Follow me, Frog!" he said, grabbing hats and scarves . . .

"What about these lights?" Bear pointed to the sky.
"Oh, Bear!" gasped Frog. They were perfect!

Back in the warm, the winter moon shone through Bear's window.

"What a magical day!" said Frog. And it wasn't over yet . . .

"Hush!" whispered Bear. "What's that jingling? It's coming from the rooftop."

Frog checked the brochure – not a THING about jingles!

"It must be Santa!" Bear exclaimed. "But we need to be asleep – quick!"

They dived under the blankets and shut their eyes tight.

"Psst, Bear! Are you sleeping? I am!" chattered Frog.

But Bear was already snoring . . .

On Christmas morning,
there was a beautifully
wrapped present by the fire.
"Bear!" squealed Frog.
"Look! It's from Santa!
He came!"

Love From Santa

They each took an end of the
ribbon and pulled.
"A sleigh!" beamed Bear.
"Why, Frog – this is
just what we need . . .

. . . for our sleigh ride!"
"SUPERSONIC!" cheered Frog.
"Can I stay again next year?
Your Christmas Hotel is the BEST!"

More FESTIVE FUN from Little Tiger Press!

It's Christmas!
Tracey Corderoy
Tim Warnes

Last Stop on the Reindeer Express
MAUDIE POWELL-TUCK · KARL JAMES MOUNTFORD

The Night Before Christmas
Clement C. Moore
Mark Marshall

Barry Timms · Ag Jatkowska
Santa to the Rescue!

When Granny SAVED Christmas
JULIA HUBERY · CAROLINE PEDLER

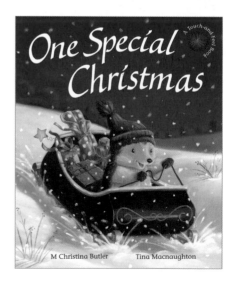

One Special Christmas
A Touch-and-Feel Book
M Christina Butler · Tina Macnaughton

For information regarding any of the above titles or for our catalogue, please contact us:
Little Tiger Press Ltd, 1 Coda Studios, 189 Munster Road, London SW6 6AW
Tel: 020 7385 6333 • E-mail: contact@littletiger.co.uk • www.littletiger.co.uk